# BRICK ADVENTURES
## 3 NEW ACTION-PACKED, ILLUSTRATED STORIES!

# STORMTROOPER CLASS CLOWNS

SCHOLASTIC INC.

Published by Scholastic Inc., *Publishers since 1920*. SCHOLASTIC and associated logos are trademarks and/or registered trademarks of Scholastic Inc.

The publisher does not have any control over and does not assume any responsibility for author or third-party websites or their content.

This book is a work of fiction. Names, characters, places, and incidents are either the product of the author's imagination or are used fictitiously, and any resemblance to actual persons, living or dead, business establishments, events, or locales is entirely coincidental.

ISBN 978-1-338-26250-6

10 9 8 7 6 5 4 3 2 1        18 19 20 21 22

Printed in the U.S.A.        40
First printing 2018

# CONTENTS

# INTRODUCTION
# Welcome to First Order School

**H**i, I'm **Kylo Ren**. I'm good at using the **Force** and even better at having cool hair! I want to tell you all about the training school we call "**First Order** School." That's where you train to join me in the First Order. Here are three stories from the recent year to think about before you apply!

# FIRST DAY AT THE FIRST ORDER

**T**oday a brand-new class of students had begun their training at First Order School! These **stormtroopers** had one goal in mind: to become great soldiers for the First Order! They needed to prove they were smart enough and evil enough to fight for Kylo Ren.

When they started school, the troopers were given classroom supplies. Each student received notebooks, folders, and blasters. They also got space pencils to take notes with. Those pencils were very important because, unlike pens, they work when there is no gravity! A trooper never knows when they might find themselves floating upside down. It's always good to be prepared.

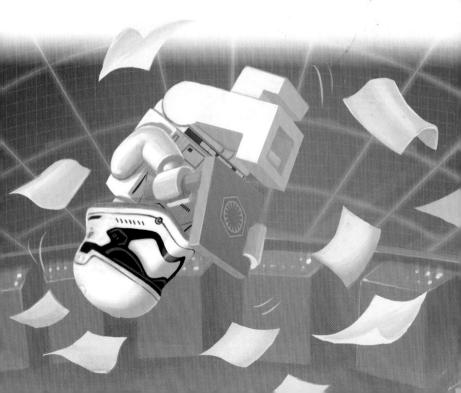

Once the students had their supplies, they gathered in homeroom. A tiny image of someone lit up at the front of the class. It was a 3-D image called a **hologram**, of **Supreme Leader Snoke**! Snoke was the leader of the First Order. He was holding a remote control that let him adjust the hologram.

"Yes, yes, I know, it's an honor to see me," Snoke said. "Sit down. Welcome to First Order School. Your training here will be fun and dangerous. And as you begin your classes, you might have questions . . ."

One of the troopers raised her hand and asked, "Sir, Supreme Leader Snoke, sir, I have a question. You are much smaller than I thought you would be."

"That is not a question!" Snoke yelled. Snoke looked at the remote control he was holding. "Now, what's going on here . . . oh darn. I set this thing to tiny mode."

With the press of a button, Snoke's hologram grew until his head nearly touched the ceiling. "Now, where was I? Ah yes. As you enter your lessons, you might have questions . . . DO NOT ASK ANY QUESTIONS! Follow my orders. And as of today, I order you to . . . enjoy yourselves."

The troopers jumped up and cheered again.

Then, with a smile, Snoke said, "Just kidding. I order you to work hard, study your helmets off, and become part of the First Order, which will wipe out the **Resistance** once and for all! But before that, you have gym class. Please join your teacher, Kylo Ren, in the **gymnasium** to begin your training."

Snoke clicked another button, and the giant hologram disappeared. Standing behind him was a very tall First Order trooper dressed in silver armor with a cape draped over her shoulder. It was **Captain Phasma**. She was one of the toughest captains of the First Order.

"Let's go, kiddos," said Phasma. "Kylo Ren doesn't like to be kept waiting. As you may have heard, patience is not what he is known for."

As the troops entered the gym, they saw that it was huge, filled with giant red First Order banners and blinking computers. In the middle of the floor, Kylo was waiting, surrounded by a bunch of metal balls! The metal balls were actually tiny **droids**.

Kylo held up one hand to get everyone's attention. A tiny droid flew up and landed in his hand. "Today, you are going to play a game called Droid Dodgeball," Kylo said. "It's just like regular dodgeball, except the balls fly around and try to zap you with a laser. If you get zapped, you're out. Last one standing wins. The game starts now!"

HELLO, CLASS . . .

All the droids flew into the air, firing lasers. Some troopers were hit right away, and an alarm sounded to tell them that they were out of the game. The troopers ran around, bumping into one another and getting hit by the lasers over and over again. Kylo thought it was very funny.

Kylo stood in the center of the room, laughing. Then, one trooper tried to use a notebook to block a laser. The laser bounced off his notepad and hit Kylo, burning his hair.

"YEE-OUCH!" he screamed. All the droids stopped immediately. They knew they'd made a big mistake. Kylo didn't like anyone messing up his cool, long hair.

Kylo turned on his red **lightsaber** and leapt after the droids. The troopers cheered as he flipped and flew through the gym and destroyed all the droids. As the last droid flew away, Kylo threw his lightsaber like a spear. The droid broke as Kylo's lightsaber smashed into the wall. But . . . his lightsaber also destroyed the gravity control in the gym. Everyone floated into the air, stuck in zero gravity.

As Kylo floated above the ground, he saw what he'd actually done to the gym. The gym was covered with wrecked droids and metal pieces.

"Students," he said while upside down. "Use your space pens to take this important note: You must never tell Supreme Leader Snoke what happened here today. This is the third gym I've destroyed this week, so let's make this our little secret. Okay?"

"Yes, sir!" the troops all cheered as they wrote in their books.

Kylo nodded. "Great. And now, for your next challenge, uh . . . rebuild the gym and clean up this mess. Actually, you should probably get used to cleaning up our messes. So, you *are* learning something important!"

# STORY #2:

# CAPTAIN PHASMA'S WILD RIDE

Every First Order trooper dreams of being a pilot. There's nothing like flying through space in a **TIE fighter** battle against a team of rebels. But before new troops face off against expert pilots, like **Poe Dameron**, they need to start small.

It was a day like any other in the halls of First Order School, and a new trooper had just been told he wasn't ready to fly yet. "No way!" he said. He flapped his arms and pretended

to zoom past his friends. "I'm ready to fly right now! Look out, **galaxy**, here I come!"

Another trooper joined in, running around the other troops: "I'm right behind you, partner!"

The two new recruits jumped down the hallway until they tripped over each other and fell. They rolled until Captain Phasma stopped them.

The fearless leader shook her head slowly. "So you think you can fly?" she asked. "Piloting a TIE fighter isn't as simple as bouncing around a hallway with your friends. If you think you're ready, then let's begin the TIE fighter driver's training course."

The troopers scrambled back to their feet and saluted Captain Phasma. "We're ready to take the wheel!"

"We will see," snapped the captain as she turned and walked toward the space deck.

The students followed her, cheering. The space deck was giant. TIE fighters and other battleships were parked on the floor and along the walls on each side. Trained First Order troopers saluted the captain as she entered the runway. At the end of the runway, an opening showed the galaxy full of stars.

WHEEEE!

"Wow," said one of the students. "I cannot believe we're about to fly an actual TIE fighter!"

"No one is actually flying a TIE fighter yet," Captain Phasma said. "You troopers didn't think that I was going to let you fly alone the very first time you set foot in a TIE fighter, did you?"

"Kind of," another student said.

"Well, then you are *kind* of wrong," said the captain. "Besides, it's trash day. There are garbage ships carrying trash outside, and you don't want to run into them. No, you will take a pretend flight, a **simulation**. We'll start with something easy, like an **asteroid belt**. Asteroids are space rocks that can hurt your ship, and you need to learn how to dodge them. It will feel like you are flying, but you will be safely tied to the space deck. The last thing we want is for any of these ships to get hurt."

One by one, the students climbed into TIE fighters that were tied to a wall. The inside of the spaceship was small. There was room for only two pilots. One pilot flew the ship, while the other was in charge of the cannons.

With the troopers aboard, Captain Phasma went to a space traffic control booth over-looking the deck to talk to the pilots. "Remember to buckle up, everyone. Safety first, even in a battle simulation."

The recruits clicked themselves into place. "Ready for action!"

"We are starting the TIE fighters now," said Captain Phasma.

Each of the TIE fighters began to hum as the engines warmed up. The troopers all cheered. "Whee! Even if we're not flying today, this is so cool!"

In the air traffic control booth, Captain Phasma ordered a trooper to prepare the asteroid battle simulation.

A trooper nodded to the captain. "Simulation ready on your command, ma'am."

"Now," said Captain Phasma, and the trooper pressed a button.

Suddenly, all of the TIE fighters blasted into space!

Phasma ran to the control booth window and watched as the training pilots flew out of sight. "Who would like to tell me why my simulation just actually launched First Order students into space without any flying experience?" she asked.

The control deck went quiet until the trooper who pressed the button spoke: "Oh, here's the problem. I hit the launch button instead of the launch *simulation* button. Hmm, maybe it's not a good idea to have those two buttons right next to each other . . . and they're the same color, too. Very confusing."

Captain Phasma yelled, "Remind me to make it less confusing for you when I get back!"

She ran out of the room and jumped inside another TIE fighter. She fired it up and flew after her new recruits, who were already far ahead of her.

"WHOA! This feels so real!" said one trooper in a pilot seat.

Another trooper reported in over the **headset**: "Hey, guys, it looks like we've reached the asteroid belt!"

A cluster of asteroids hovered outside of his front windshield as the trooper took the steering controls. He swerved down, barely missing the first rock chunk. He weaved the ship in and out of giant **boulders**. "Wow, if this was real, I'd be so scared right now!" he said.

Another voice interrupted their radios: "All recruits stay where you are and do not, under any circumstances, shift into **hyperdrive**, unless you want to never fly again!"

"Uh-oh, that's Captain Phasma," said one trooper. "And she does not sound happy."

Suddenly, a net swooped over the ships and pulled them safely from the asteroid belt. The same net caught each and every TIE fighter that had a First Order student inside. As the pilots looked up, they saw the net attached to another TIE fighter, which expertly flew through space. Captain Phasma sat in the pilot's seat.

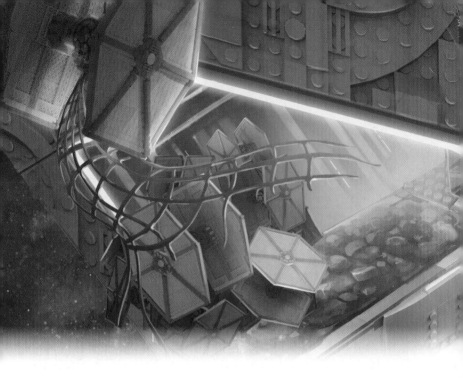

"Now I need to get you all back before Kylo knows we're missing," Captain Phasma told the others.

But when they were almost back to the space deck, another giant ship took off—a huge trash ship! The captain of the giant ship turned quickly to avoid them, but she couldn't get out of the way in time. All the TIE fighters plunged deep into a pile of trash aboard the garbage ship.

Back on the space deck, Kylo Ren had just arrived to see what all the commotion was about. He waved to Captain Phasma as she exited her filthy TIE fighter.

"I never thought your flying stunk, Phasma," said Kylo as he coughed at the smell. "But you are out to prove me wrong."

Captain Phasma held her head high. "I might not have the best of luck when it comes to landing in garbage," she said, "but I always live to fight another day!"

# STORY #3:

## The Best *Worst* Villain

**W**hile training to fight **Wookiees** and rebels might sound dangerous, it's nothing compared to lunchtime at First Order School. The troopers are treated to three meals a day, prepared by the worst cooks in the galaxy.

One day at lunch, two students stared at their awful food. On their trays, a dusty piece of bread floated in a sea of green glop.

"What is this supposed to be?" asked one of the troopers.

"According to the menu, it's macaroni and cheese," said the other trooper. She couldn't believe the bad smell coming from such a small amount of food. "Ugh, what are they trying to do to us by feeding us this disgusting gunk?"

"Good question," said the first trooper. "It's like they give us this horrible stuff on purpose. Maybe this nasty food is supposed to make us meaner, angrier, and every bit as bitter as what's on our trays?"

EEEWW . . .

The second trooper nodded in agreement. "It's like they say: 'You are what you eat.' And if we eat the most evil food, then we'll become the most evil troopers ever. It could even be part of our training!"

The first trooper lifted the spoon up to his mouth before stopping and letting the food drop back down. "Gah, I can't eat it," he said. "Since when is macaroni and cheese green? And sure, our armor is stain resistant, but if I spill any of this food on me, I'll never get the smell out."

"Yeah, I know," the second trooper said. "You know who probably loves this stuff? Kylo Ren. He's so evil he probably thinks this slop tastes as sweet as candy."

The other trooper shook his head. "That's where you're wrong. **General Hux** probably eats way more gross food than Kylo Ren. He is way more evil than Kylo. He commands the First Order army, and he blew up an entire star system!"

"That is pretty evil," said the trooper as she pushed the food around her tray. "But Kylo Ren destroyed the Jedi. That was also pretty evil."

"I suppose we'll never know who is more evil, Kylo Ren or General Hux," the first trooper admitted. "Unless we see them eat this food!"

The two troopers jumped up and ran across the **cafeteria** searching for Kylo and Hux. They found both of the leaders sitting at a table together. Kylo had his mask off as he talked to Hux. Neither of them expected the troopers to interrupt their lunch, which was way better than what the troopers ate.

"Excuse me, your villainous sirs," the first trooper said. "My friend and I have a question for you both. We were wondering which of you is the evilest of all?"

The leaders looked at each other and laughed.

"That has to be the worst question I've ever heard," said General Hux. "Wouldn't you agree, Kylo?"

"Definitely the worst question," said Kylo. "I'm the evilest villain of all. Everyone knows that."

Suddenly, General Hux's laughter stopped. "Oh, Kylo, don't be so silly. I'm the evilest **villain** of all. Sure, you are mysterious, moody, and you have the whole Force thing working for you, but at the end of the day, I'm the biggest bad guy around here."

A crowd of troopers gathered around the leaders' lunch table. This was the most interesting thing to ever happen in the First Order cafeteria.

"It sounds like we need to have a contest to prove, once and for all, who is the evilest," suggested Kylo.

"You're on!" said Hux. "What should we do to prove who's better at being the worst?"

The first trooper waved his arm in the air. "I know! I know! You can eat the cafeteria lunch today! Whoever finishes first has to be the most vile villain ever."

At this suggestion, Kylo and Hux both gagged and turned as green as the macaroni and cheese.

"I've got a better idea," Kylo announced. "We'll have three challenges, and the winner is the worst. First, I challenge you to a scare game, Hux. Whoever scares the most troopers wins."

General Hux cracked a crooked smile. "I'll go first. Any trooper in this room who isn't scared right now will be forced to clean out the cafeteria kitchen . . . and take out the trash for a week!"

A **quivering** gasp filled the room as every trooper's stomach collectively let out a gross gurgle.

"That settles that," said Hux. "I'm clearly the winner here."

"Not so fast." Kylo reached under the table, and in one swift move, he put on his mask and turned on his lightsaber. The **jagged** edge of its red blade heated up the room and scared several troopers out of their actual **uniforms**—helmets, pants, and all!

Even General Hux flinched with fear.

"Point, Kylo Ren," the **cloaked** leader said in a distorted voice from underneath his mask. "The second challenge is up to you, Hux."

The general smoothed back his red hair. "Let's have a good, old-fashioned race, then. The first evildoer to cross the finish line wins. Troopers, form a finish line at the end of the lunchroom. We will break through you to win."

"What does a race have to do with being evil?" asked Kylo Ren.

"Line up at the starting point here and find out." General Hux bent into a racing position. "Unless you're too scared to race me?"

Kylo put his lightsaber away and leapt over the table, landing right next to Hux. "I'm not afraid of a footrace."

The troopers counted off all together: "On your mark, get set, GO!"

Kylo Ren bolted into an early lead by using the Force to freeze General Hux for a moment. But the general was fast—just as Kylo almost reached the finish line, Hux grabbed Ren's hood and tossed him backward. Kylo Ren landed on his bottom with a thud as Hux ran to victory, crashing through the troopers and knocking all of them down like bowling pins.

The troopers knew that using the Force to win was evil, but Hux using Ren's own fancy outfit to win the race and humiliate him added insult to injury.

"Looks like we're tied," said General Hux. "There's only one challenge left: a **duel**."

"A lightsaber duel?" Kylo laughed. "You have got to be kidding. I'd take you down faster than you took me down in that race."

"No, a blaster duel," explained General Hux. "We'll set up targets and whoever blasts the most will win."

"Or you could just eat the food," suggested the first trooper.

"A blaster duel it is!" both Hux and Kylo said at the same time.

General Hux went first, ordering several troopers to hold their cafeteria trays above their heads as targets. Hux quickly blasted the center of each tray. The troopers all cheered, even the ones who now had green macaroni and cheese spilled all over them.

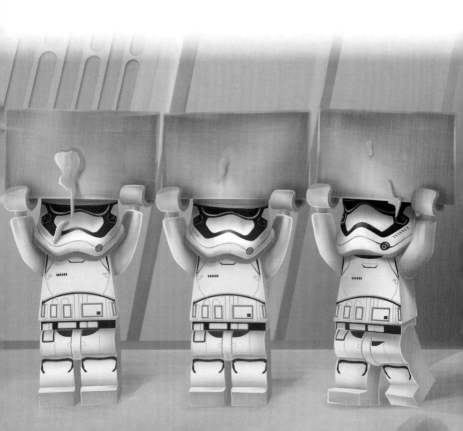

"Your turn, Kylo," said General Hux as he motioned for the green-slimed troopers to raise several more tray targets.

"I thought this was supposed to be a challenge," said Kylo as he pulled off his mask. "Hitting targets with your eyes open is one thing, but doing it with your eyes closed is something else."

Placing his helmet down, Kylo Ren shut his eyes and fired, with the Force guiding his aim. He struck the first four targets but missed the fifth! His final blast bounced off the lunchroom walls until it hurled back into the kitchen and exploded.

The room went silent. Then, Hux laughed. "What a rotten shot that was, Kylo! You missed the last target completely!"

Kylo Ren winked. "Did I?" he asked. "Let's ask the troopers. Did I miss my target, or did I just **annihilate** the awful food you have to eat every day?"

The First Order students swarmed in and lifted Kylo on their shoulders. "Three cheers for Kylo Ren, the destroyer of bad cafeteria food!"

"Sorry, Hux," said Ren as he turned on his lightsaber again. "It looks like the troops pick me. Okay, everyone, we're ordering out for lunch! Who likes pizza? I can slice it up for you!"

# THE END

# GLOSSARY

**ANNIHILATE:** To completely defeat.

**ASTEROID BELT:** A group of rocks found in outer space.

**BOULDER:** A big, round rock.

**CAFETERIA:** A place to eat where food is served at a counter and then taken to tables.

**CAPTAIN PHASMA:** A female stormtrooper commander who works under Kylo Ren and General Hux.

**CLOAK:** A long, loose piece of outer clothing.

**DROID:** A type of mechanical robot used for chores and other tasks.

**DUEL:** A fight between two people.

**FIRST ORDER:** An evil group led by Supreme Leader Snoke that wants to take over the galaxy.

**FORCE:** An invisible energy that binds the universe together and can be used by those who are Force-sensitive to move objects or sense attacks before they happen.

**GALAXY:** All the stars and planets where the events in *Star Wars* take place.

**GENERAL HUX:** The leader of the First Order army.

**GYMNASIUM:** A large, indoor room used for sports.

**HEADSET:** A device used to hold an earphone and microphone to someone's face, letting them talk to and listen to others.

**HOLOGRAM:** A 3-D picture made using light.

**HYPERDRIVE:** A system that lets spaceships fly faster than the speed of light, so they can move between very long distances in a short period of time.

**JAGGED:** Having sharp or uneven surfaces.

**KYLO REN:** A Force user and former Jedi trainee who left the Jedi to join the First Order.

**LIGHTSABER:** A laser sword used by people who also use the Force.

**POE DAMERON:** A commander in the Resistance who is a very good pilot.

**QUIVER:** To shake all over.

**RESISTANCE:** A small force led by General Leia Organa created to fight the First Order.

**SIMULATION:** A pretend exercise of something that looks like it's real.

**STORMTROOPER:** Soldiers of the First Order.

**SUPREME LEADER SNOKE:** The leader of the First Order and powerful user of the dark side of the Force.

**TIE FIGHTER:** The star fighter spaceship used by the First Order.

**UNIFORM:** A set of clothing given out to a group that is the same for everyone in the group.

**VILLAIN:** A character who fights against heroes.

**WOOKIEE:** A tall, hairy creature. Chewbacca is a famous Wookiee.

# LEGO® BRICK ADVENTURES

## ENJOY THESE OTHER
## LEGO BRICK ADVENTURES TITLES!